Two Women and a Nightengale

MICHAEL BETANCOURT

Wildside Press

Wildside Press

1www.wildsidepress.com

a novel in collage

after Max Ernst

CHAPTER 1

wherein Rose begins her journey

Once there were two sisters, Marcella and Rose, who both loved the Nightengale. But Marcella was jealous with her music and made Nightengale say . . .

"The time has come for me to adieu to you. Farewell, Rose, I must fly away to seek the knowledge of the Moon." And he was gone, blown over in the night.

Despairing in the morning sun, Rose sat and watched her pet fish fly, then took flight herself to follow her flighty love . . .

leaving Marcella at the gate barking, "Come back here right now, or I'll get you with my magic mop and" . . .

"that should put your Nightengale in perspective!"

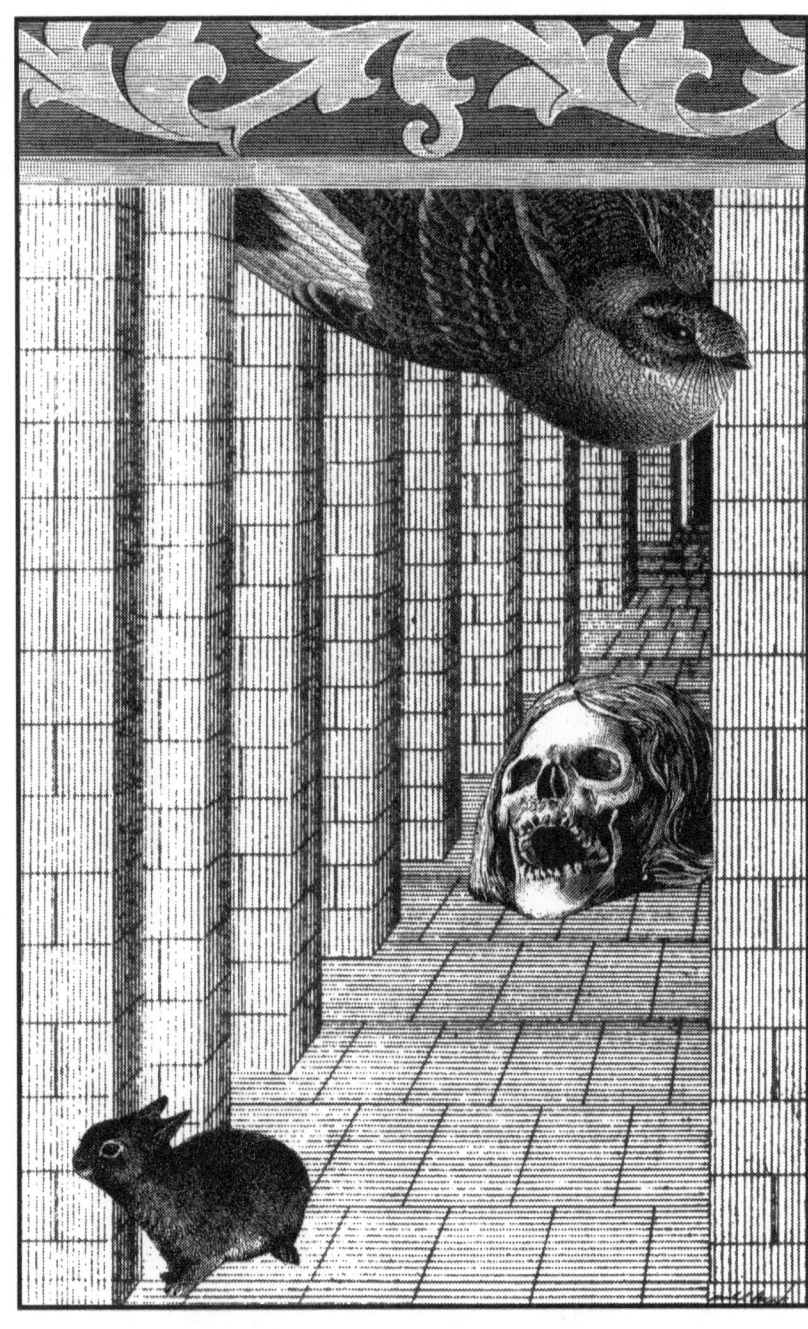

"But sister," cried Rose, "my hands have touched clouds and washed in the falling water near" . . .

"the Wading Machine and the sea where mothers drown their naughty sons! It is not for me to return, for" . . .

"the tide is rushing in. Sing a silent prayer for me as I fly out to see!" Her wings beat a merry jig, but when she saw . . .

the Hôtel Sur La Mer, and realized the candle was burning low into the briny waters. She went inside and saw . . .

the lobby was a hustle-bustle of activity and song, with people riposting, lunging, and parrying in time to the music. But . . .

nevertheless, the Porter saw her and, (ignoring the storm foaming at the window), carried her up to a room where . . .

she hid her face from the Moon, and . . .

dreamed of swimming with the wise sea turtles, (who in mock despair),
swam with her up, up, up . . .

to land and warn her, "Those among them who are merry sometimes turn their behind to the sky, but strike their own bellies lightly!"

Then they boarded their black boat and . . .

left her to lie and rust on the beach.

Meanwhile . . .

CHAPTER 2

wherein Marcella begins her pursuit

Marcella, her head swollen with rage, scared the town watchtower by starting a fire with her club mates, before retiring for cola mid-afternoon.

But it was that evening . . .

that she decided to sneak past the busy minors and enter the Brat Cave where she would go when she really wanted to debug Rose. And off she went . . .

in her roach coach, flying magically over the hill pond and the bird woman named Al Cat Razz, to . . .

turn left to fly out to see the way Rose went out to sea.

The night passed away . . .

very quickly, leaving Marcella alone to fly past the last marker and into the sky that . . .

crosses the Sea of Flying Books whose bindings grew feathery with the damp, and their pages heavy with secret forebodings . . .

to the Island of Music where she decided to beach her roach coach in a ditch.

But up the rise . . .

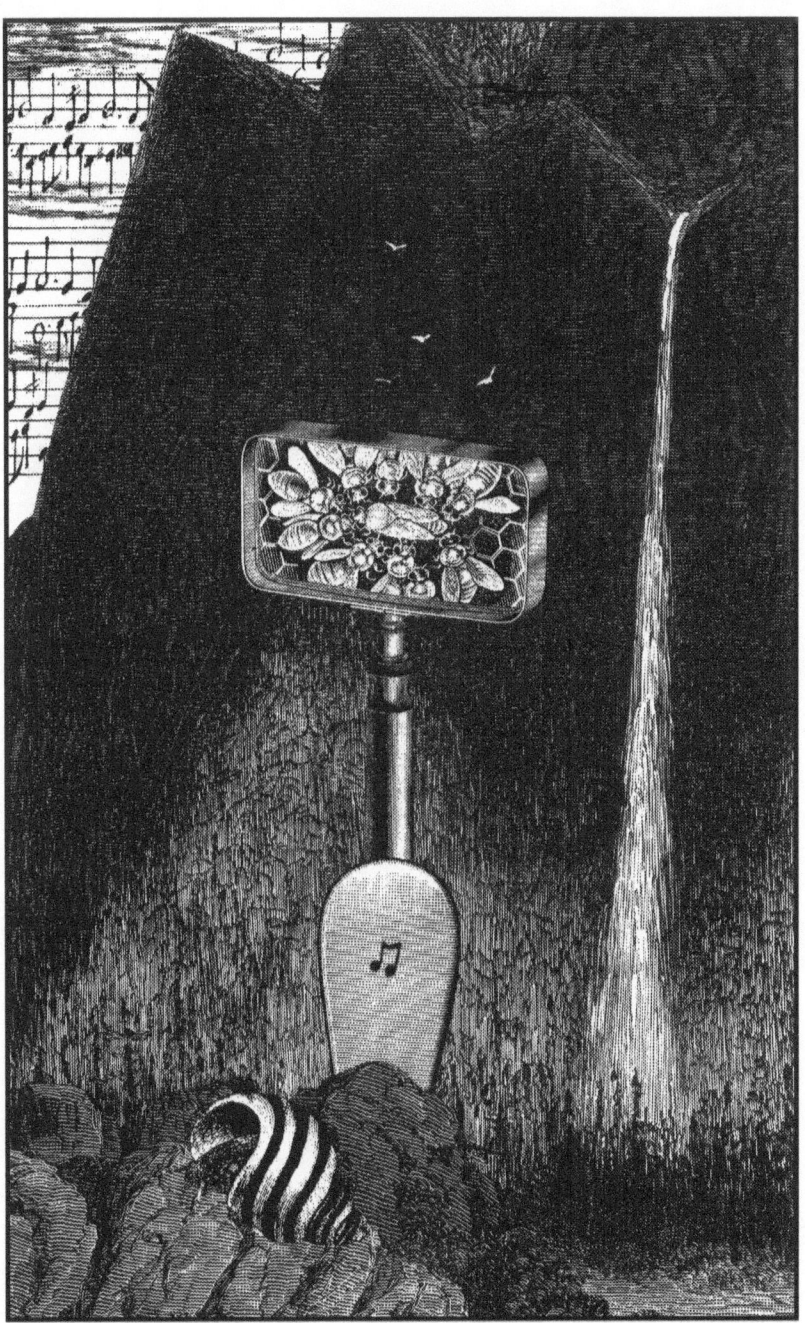

the Organs of the C glistened wetly, hooting over the surf for bits of cauliflower and broccoli. They ignored her in their festiveness . . .

and Marcella wandered silently inland and set up her tent just as a dreadful great rock concert began with a heavy shower of notes, forcing her to take up dancing for the night.

But the Nightengale . . .

CHAPTER 3

the travels of the Nightengale

knew nothing of any of this as he flew beyond the Valley of Shears and over the sharp points of the sheer cliff's face . . .

and down the other side, following the night breeze that whispers softly, "Buy twelve doves and get next door to a lark," and on, down into the valley beyond . . .

the Sinking Venus, where little men come to unlook and unlearn her secrets, and beyond. . .

the Nightengale flew over the Clock Graveyard, those tombs sinking
quietly before the dank waters where . . .

the great Panopticon of Err bloats darkly . . .

and the State's Altar with its horny gate opens onto the Sea of Tranquility.

But . . .

CHAPTER 4

Rose awakens on her journey

as the day unfolded like a white table cloth, and Rose checked out the morning after . . .

her excellent breakfast briskly conducted by the Maitre d' and his Symphony of Rats, she . . .

watched the dark clouds gathering along the horizon, collecting stardust as Dawn played over the calm morning waters.

    Rose flew east, over . . .

the turbulent ceaseless seas around the Flat Islands, whose waters were stirred by . . .

the flatulence that kept the islands afloat. But, in the distance beyond the islands, she saw . . .

the Great Hot Continental rise, with its famously steamy water. And when she reached the beach, she . . .

decided to take a bath, but she was interrupted by a strange bird that said to her:

"A pair of silk stockings is not a leap into space, but the stones are full of entrails that lead to the Moon" . . .

"where the guy's air rises into space!" And Rose took its clear advice, flying suddenly . . .

UP! UP! UP!

And away into the world of dreams . . .

to arrive at the Moon, her destination.

Meanwhile . . .

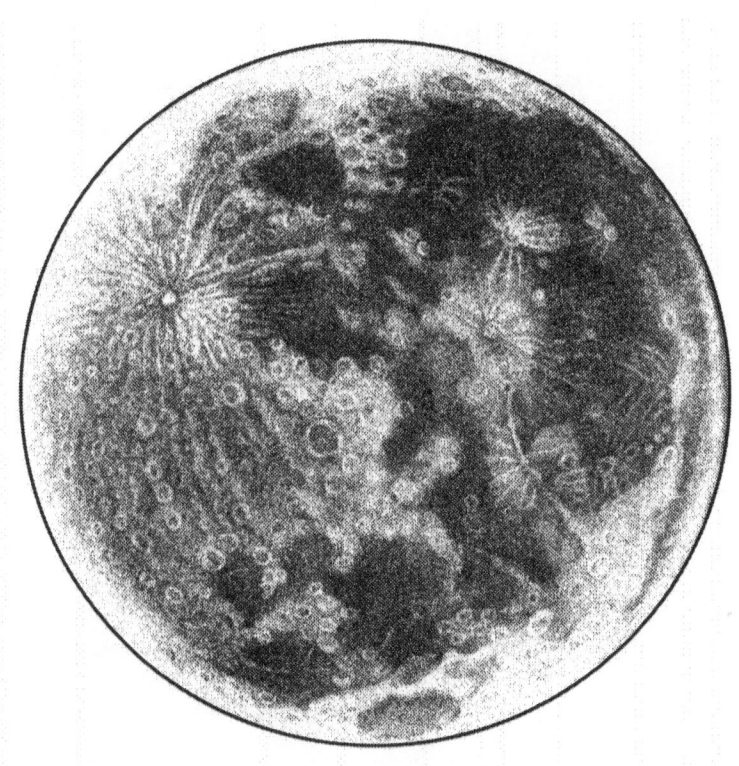

CHAPTER 5

Finalé & Revelation

Marcella flew around the Island of Music, passing over a strange whale dance, to . . .

drive her roach coach toward, then through, the Moongate that loomed
among the pipes on the beach . . .

and streak over the Moon's famous Green Cheese like a comet.
Until . . .

she found a nice parking place, and went to search for her sister, Rose, who . . .

had just been visiting the Mad Man of the Moon, who'd given her a box of fruit-flavored condoms. Rose was busy carrying them away, when suddenly . . .

she was startled by a voice in the sky. She looked up who it was to see the Starfish rising into the night.

It said to her . . .

"Laughter is dying among the machines who bake the sky, but I will search the heavens for spare change. Would you care to join me?"

(Rose's reply: "No, not at the moment, but thank you anytime. I'm searching for my unremitted love.")

And . . .

sometime later, Rose saw him flying off and away as she rocked her
honorific path, so she . . .

called out for him.

Hearing her plaintiff cry, he turned high in the night sky, (passing the Forgetting Machine), to . . .

come down and join with her under the Dover Special Edition Cliffs. But Marcella heard her cry too, and . . .

came running, fists waving high in the night sky, shouting to Rose . . .

"Oh, my sister, that is the very bird that came and threatened us as children! Did you knot your rope in forgetfulness?"

Rose turned in anger, but knew Marcella was true, so . . .